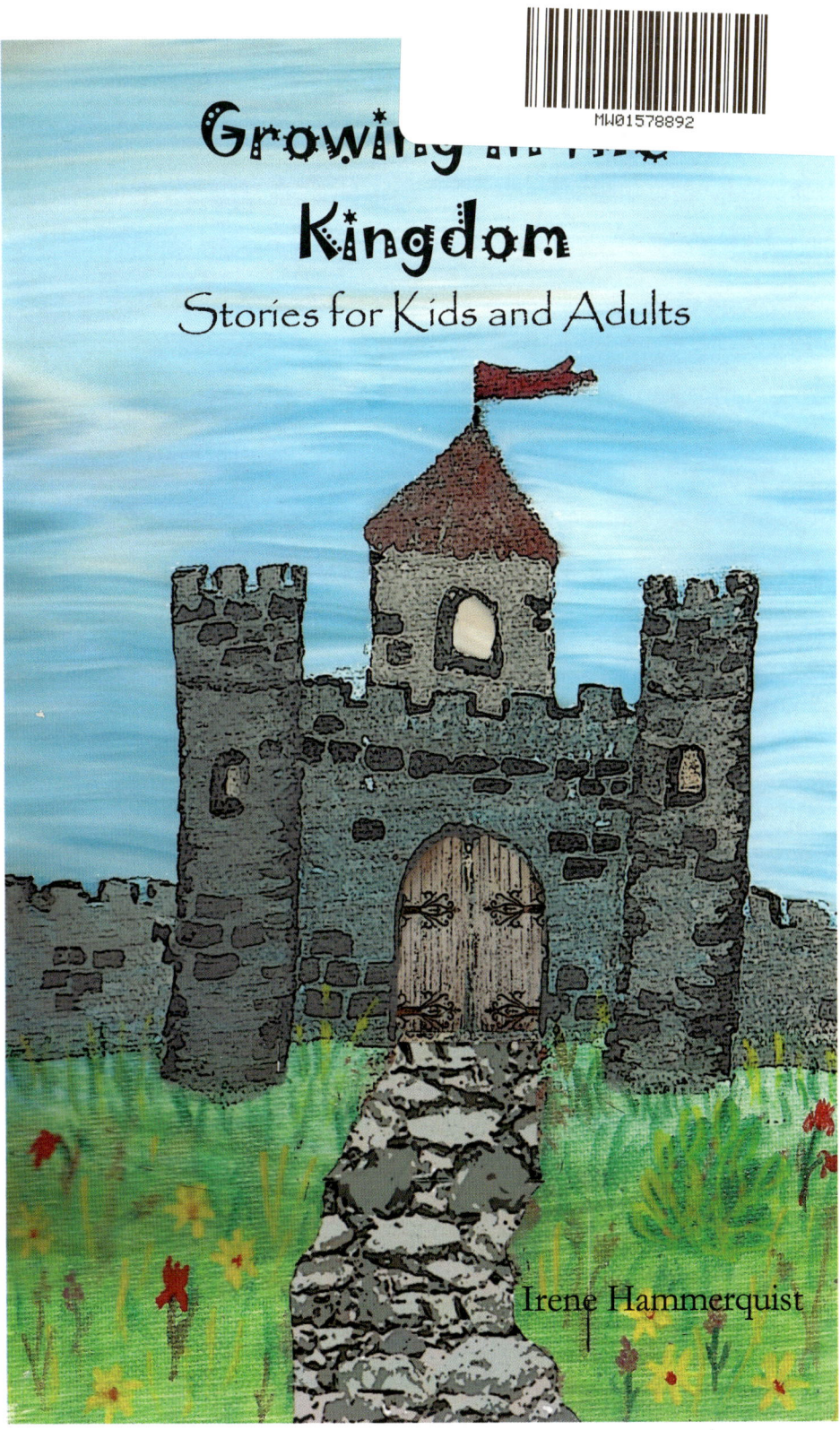

Growing in the Kingdom
Stories for Kids and Adults

Irene Hammerquist

Copyright © 2012 Irene Hammerquist

All rights reserved.

ISBN-10:1500611573
ISBN-13:9781500611576

DEDICATION

To my husband, Don, and to all seven of my children, Kyle, Stephanie, Courtney, Kurt, Chris, Jeanna, and Deanna who live their lives pursuing a deeper relationship with the King.

CONTENTS

	Acknowledgments	i
1	Dancing Delight	1
2	Royal Knight	5
3	Painting Right	11
4	Spreading Light	15
5	Wisdom's Sight	19

ACKNOWLEDGMENTS

Thanks to my dad and mom who allowed me the freedom to be who God created me to be. Thanks to my husband, Don, a constant stronghold, encouragement and support throughout the entire process. Thanks to my children who endured hearing the story read and re-read numerous times, too many to count. I bet your glad it's done! And thanks especially to God for never giving up on me, even when I doubted myself, and for blessing me with a portion of His creative spirit.

1 DANCING DELIGHT

There once was a kingdom ruled by a good and kind king. He visited his people often, and they would stop what they were doing and run to greet him. The king enjoyed talking to them and spending time with them. He played and danced in the meadow with the children. When the people called him, he would come and meet with them. The king made sure they had everything they needed. Many times the king sent his son to bring special gifts to his people. The people were happy and rejoiced with one another, sharing all they had been given. People would drop by the palace just to say "hi" to the king. Their children would dance in his courts with joy and laughter, waving flags and singing. The kingdom grew and prospered under the king's protection and in his love.

Over time, the people began to desire the gifts more than the king who gave them. The people became jealous when the king gave gifts to others. They no longer shared the gifts they were given, but rather hid them away. The people began to think that they had to earn the gifts by doing something extra or by doing an especially good job. They worked very hard to earn the king's approval and acceptance.

The king was very sad. All he wanted was to love his people and have them love him. He never meant for them to work for his gifts. He loved them and thought of them like his children. He just plain liked giving them surprises. He liked seeing the joy and delight in their eyes. The king enjoyed spending time with his people.

The people only tried even harder. Some began to use the king as a tool to persuade others to work harder. They told their children, "You better do good, the king is always watching." As time went on, people actually began to believe that all the king cared about was how much they did and how good their work was. People stopped running out to greet the king. Instead, they hid in shame. The children began to fear the king. As the children grew and made mistakes, as all children do, they believed they would never be good enough. They couldn't possibly be acceptable to the king. They feared being punished or scolded and stopped going out to see him. Playing and dancing in the meadow with the king became a lost memory. Most thought and talked about it as a fantasy or dream that they would never be able to earn.

The king looked out the window of his castle and tears welled up in his eyes. He longed for a relationship with his people. He so wanted to invite them to his castle and see the children dancing in his courts again. His heart ached to see his people become great men and women in the kingdom. But this stubborn group, how could he get them to put aside their pride and embrace his love?

As the king gazed out the window toward the meadow, a spark of hope and longing made its way from what he saw to the very depths of his heart. His heart leapt with joy. A smile spread across his face as he watched her. There in the meadow with arms held out in front of her, was a little girl pretending to dance with someone. How precious she was spinning and twirling through the tall grass and flowers to the songs of the birds. The blue sky with its pink and yellow streaks of light looked like a painted canvas of color in stark contrast to the small girl's drab, tattered brown dress. Even the meadow was bright with colorful wild flowers peeking through a sea of golden grass. Yet to  the king it was a perfect image, an image that stirred something deep within. Joy that had been bottled up inside threatened to bubble up and overflow.

Could it be? Had she heard stories of the king dancing in the meadow with the children? Could she be imagining that she was dancing with the king?

Down in the meadow, the child danced to a song that played cadence in her mind and heart.

"I love the king and he loves me.

When I call to him, he comes to me.

Someday I'll dance in his palace strong.

I'll dance with the king all day long."

In her imagination, she pictured herself dancing with the king. Her drab brown dress had been traded in for a beautiful white gown with ribbon and lace. She imagined him smiling at her.

The girl was totally focused on her daydream. Perhaps it was because of this, that she didn't hear the hoof beats, nor did she see the king slide off his horse at the edge of the meadow. Her intense focus on the imaginary scene caused her to miss seeing the solitary tear that escaped the king's eye and slowly made its way down his handsome chiseled cheek.

The child was suddenly overwhelmed with sadness. She sank to her knees, the grief too much to bear. She buried her tear streaked face in her hands. Her body shook with the sobs coming from deep within. She cried for a dream that would never be. Her heart longed to be loved by a king she had never met. The tears pouring from her eyes could not wash away her desire and longing to dance in the king's courts. Why dream if dreams were never meant to become real?

As she wept, the king quietly approached the child. Tears streamed down his face as his heart felt her pain and loving compassion exploded from deep in his heart. He knelt down beside her and asked, "what's wrong child?"

Like flood gates being opened after a spring storm, her words tumbled out. "I'll never be good enough. I try so hard but I just can't seem to do things right. I'm not smart enough, pretty enough, or good enough. I yell and get angry sometimes. My clothes are shabby and torn. Yet, I just want the king!"

The king wrapped his arms around the young girl and gave her a teddy bear hug. As his strong arms enfolded her small frame, peace and joy washed over her body, mind, and thoughts. This was a feeling she had never felt before. She looked up into this strangers face through blurry eyes. She squinted; somehow he looked familiar like she should recognize him, but his identity remained hidden. Then he smiled at her and spoke her name. Like a light bulb flashing on, she knew. This man was the king.

He took her hand and helped her up saying, "Rise up and be crowned with glory and grace." The king placed a wreath of wild flowers on her head. Then the king scooped her up in his strong arms and they danced all around the meadow. After dancing and playing, the king told her that he loved her. Time didn't seem to matter. The little girl was filled with joy just sitting there in the meadow's grass with the king. She pinched herself to be sure she wasn't dreaming. She wanted this moment to last forever. She was in the presence of the king. He said she was welcome in his castle anytime. The king looked lovingly at the little girl and told her she was his little princess and more than worthy to dance in his courts.

The sun crept behind a small gray cloud that hung low on the horizon. It was getting late. As the king mounted his horse, he promised to answer whenever she called. The girl turned and started skipping home just as a late afternoon storm began to shower the kingdom. Even rain couldn't dampen her joyful spirit. She found something that could fill the empty place in her little heart. She had found the king – or rather – he had found her.

The rain felt refreshing as the king rode back to the castle. Light shone around him as if coming out of his very pores. He was so happy that he couldn't help but hum to the beat of the horse's hooves. He loved his people, and this little girl – she loved him. The tide was turning.

After that day, the king met many times with the girl. He even nicknamed her his little "Dancing Delight". She brought her friends and the time spent with the king in the meadow was enjoyed by all the children. As the children grew in their love for the king and one another, they began to influence those around them.

2 ROYAL KNIGHT

He noticed them in the meadow many times. The king and the children looked so happy together. He would watch them from behind a tree at the edge of the meadow wishing he were younger so he could be a part of them. As he watched he wondered if he would ever fit in anywhere, somewhere. Then he would return to practicing shooting his bow and using his sword. His sword was made of wood, but it was the right weight to practice with. One time he went so far as to creep behind a large rock by the stream. From this vantage point, he could hear the deep musical sound of the king's voice.

This kingdom he lived in wasn't bad; it just wasn't always good either. People talked about the old days when the king used to come around a lot. But they didn't realize it was their own selfish ways and desires that now kept the king at a distance. They wanted things their way and didn't have time for the king. Until recently even the children had never met the king. If the king had started coming back sooner, maybe the boy could have met him in the meadow. Nobody else had seen the king when he scooped the little girl up in his arms and placed a wreath on her head. But the boy, he had watched from the edge of the meadow yearning for it to be him. He had noticed over the next few weeks how more and more children came to meet with the king. The adults thought the kids were just playing and were happy to have a few minutes to themselves.

Now, here he was. And, oh what a glorious sound was the king's laughter. It stirred something deep inside the boy's heart. He stretched his head out further for a better view. He thought the king glanced his way and in shame and embarrassment he ducked back into the trees. His weapons coach had made it very clear that the king only chose the best, the most fit and the most accurate archers and swordsmen to defend his kingdom. He looked into the image reflected in the small stream in the trees. What he saw was nothing to brag about. He was short for his age and scrawny in comparison to the other boys. As he gazed at his reflection, he saw himself as a stick with a head, hardly champion material.

Over the years, many young men from the town had tried to be accepted into the ranks of the king's army. Sadly, most had returned. The town assumed that they weren't good enough and had been rejected by the king. The young men, feeling embarrassed, went back to their old lives with their heads hung in shame. They never talked about why they had been turned down, so the cycle of rejection continued. The boy, even now was comparing himself to these young men. In his own eyes, he always came up wanting. He would never measure up.

The king noticed the boy behind the rock as he twirled and danced with the children. On the next spin, he shot a glance in that direction hoping to smile at the boy. But that was not to be. The boy avoided looking at him and shrunk back into the trees.

Why? Why did this people heap shame and judgment on these children? They viewed everything through the looking glasses of rules and performance. The town people believed the young men who returned did not perform to the king's standards. In reality, performance had little to do with it. The king looked at their heart calling. He knew what they were destined for, some teachers, some doctors and others representatives to the king. He knew what was best for each one. He could work with anyone who had a heart devoted to him. But, the king loved these boys too much to place them in his army because their dad or the town wanted it. Some of these young men were destined for greatness, just in other things. Unfortunately, they were being held back by the rejection placed on them by the town people who viewed other callings as less important.

This boy, he was different. The king saw his heart. He looked longingly at the king and the children. He possessed the heart of a valiant warrior, a dread champion, a heart full of love and trust. He had a heart to serve and an amazing capacity to love and show compassion. The king would look out of the throne room window every day and watch the boy. As he gazed out toward the meadow, he saw the boy practicing. The king enjoyed his daily ritual and was amazed and excited to see the boy's growth and improvement.

When the king met with the children in the meadow, he would arrive early and leave a note or little surprise on the rock by the stream. One note simply said, "You are awesome." The boy found the notes and treats, but couldn't believe they were actually for him. Oh, he wanted to believe it, but who would care about a scrawny little kid with a dream too big for his small stature. Who left the note? The boy wondered and thought about it as he practiced. He brought an old wooden box from home, put the treasured items in it, and hid it in the hollow of a tree that stood near the rock. He didn't want to be accused of stealing the things, but the notes and surprises made him feel special. He couldn't just leave them there to be blown away by the wind or damaged by the rain.

Then one day a note was left that had his name on it. His little heart leapt inside his chest. Could it be? Had the notes and treats really been meant for him? A breath-catching excitement danced in his inner most being and crept up his throat and spine. He let out a quiet squeal of delight as he imagined that the gifts had been left by the king himself. He looked again at the hand-written note. The handwriting was neat and graceful looking. The boy realized then that he hadn't even read a single word past his name. He leaned back against the rock to support his trembling frame as he began to read the note.

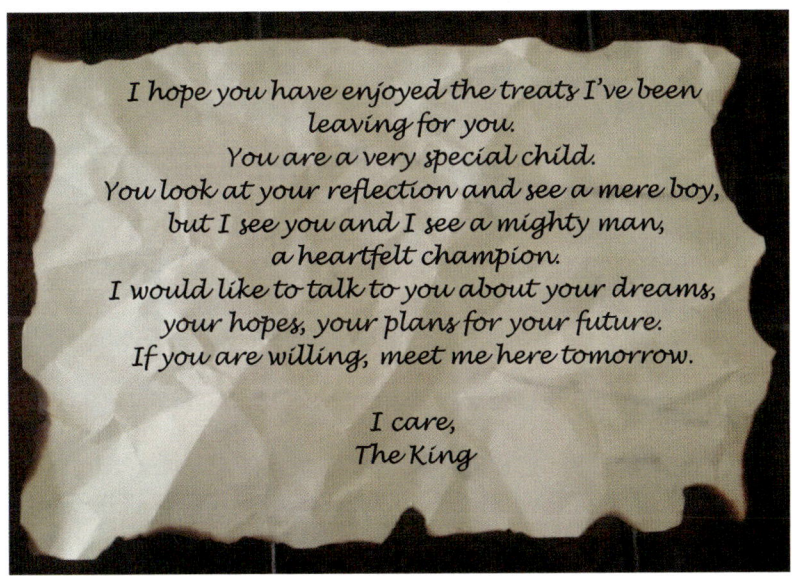

I hope you have enjoyed the treats I've been leaving for you.
You are a very special child.
You look at your reflection and see a mere boy,
but I see you and I see a mighty man,
a heartfelt champion.
I would like to talk to you about your dreams,
your hopes, your plans for your future.
If you are willing, meet me here tomorrow.

I care,
The King

Tears were flowing down the boy's face as he read the words that had been lovingly written by the king. He brushed them away with the back of his hand. He wasn't sure why he was even crying. He was excited, yet scared. He tucked the note into his pocket and headed home. He needed to get ready for tomorrow. He would meet the king.

The king noticed the boy's smile and the skip in his step as he left the meadow. The joy that he felt with the children was now turning into pure elation. He laughed deeper, he smiled bigger, he would talk to the boy tomorrow.

As the boy headed back to town and throughout the rest of the evening, doubt crept into his heart and planted its wicked seed. He had a dream that the older boys in town had written the note to get a laugh. Would they be waiting there tomorrow to ridicule him? They already thought he was foolish for even trying to join the king's army. They called him names and made fun of him. His insecurity and poor self-image fed the seed. He didn't really understand who he was and the potential that he had.

As the sun dawned bright and spread its warm rays across the kingdom, the boy looked out his window deep in thought. What if the note really was from the king, then not going would be turning down the king. If the note was from the boys, then he would have to endure the teasing and jeering laughter if he went. He would just have to chance it. Something in the note stirred a longing in his heart.

As he approached the meadow, the boy was very quiet – listening. He slipped from tree trunk to tree trunk so as not to be seen. As he peered around the trunk of the closest tree, his heart skipped a beat. There stood the king. He approached slowly, not wanting to startle the king who seemed deep in thought. As his small frame came out from behind the tree, the king jumped up, ran to the boy and swung him into the air. With a joyous sounding voice he whispered, "I knew you would come." They went and sat on a rock dangling their feet in the stream. The boy felt happy, no, bigger than happy, no this was bigger than big. The king wanted to talk to him.

The king looked at the boy and said, "I meant what I said in the letter. You are a mighty man, you can be a valiant warrior if you want to and I would be honored for you to serve in my ranks." The boy looked at the king, shame came over his face. In a tiny quiet voice he uttered, "I almost didn't come. I was afraid." The king put his arm around the boy's shoulders. "I know," he said, "you doubted it was really me and feared being teased. But please understand, there was no other way. It had to be your choice. I know your heart, but I also know you've been hurt. It had to be your choice to leave the hurt and fear behind." A smile crept from cheek to cheek. "I will, I will leave it all behind," the boy exclaimed, as he leapt into the king's arms and gave him a hug.

The king met with the boy often after that day. They hung out together and the king helped the boy refine his skills. The words of love and encouragement filled the boy's heart and he began to see all that he could do and be. The king referred to him as his "little dread champion" and the seed of belief started growing in place of the fear and doubt. Even the older boys in town started looking at him differently. Something about him had changed, but they weren't sure what. The boy knew what had changed, he had chosen the king, or rather, the king had chosen him.

The king enjoyed the boy and the innocence that flowed from him. This boy would become a champion that the enemy would not want to contend with. He was the king's very own "royal knight". As he spoke the words of the name he now called the boy, he knew it would be. A sparkle lit his eyes every time he thought of the boy. How good it was to let hope live and to see dreams become reality. The tides weren't just turning, a wave was growing.

3 PAINTING RIGHT

The king noticed a spark of light reflecting off something up on the hillside above the meadow. As he gazed out of the window of his castle, he stared in that direction watching the sporadic sparks of light. The children had told him that a crazy artist lived up there. He knew who they were talking about. She wasn't crazy; it was just that the town people didn't understand her art. She always painted pictures depicting stories of a king who visited the people long ago. She had never actually saw the king, but she dreamed about the stories and then painted what she saw in her dreams. The town people thought it nothing more than useless fantasy that would displease the king. He would like to talk to her. But right now, he was just glancing over his kingdom. He loved his people, but they had convinced themselves that the king only cared about how good they were. They had stopped coming out to see him long ago. Now, most of the people had never even met the king. Change was happening however. Ever since he had met the little girl in the meadow, the group of children that came to visit with him had increased. Then he had met the boy who wanted to serve in his army. That boy caused the atmosphere to change everywhere he went.

Just then a series of glinting light drew his attention back to the hillside. She must be really focused on painting. He smiled to himself as he thought of what their first encounter might be like. She didn't know how accurately her paintings of the king had captured his appearance. Wouldn't she be shocked if he walked up to her? Yes, he would go and see her.

Up on the hillside, the artist glanced down at the meadow and then back to her canvas. She had seen the children gathering in the meadow with some man. It was fun to watch them dance and play. She had been looking down at the meadow the day that man came riding up on a horse. What a beautiful horse it was! She had painted some pictures of it in the following weeks. One picture held the image of the king from her dreams mounted on that regal horse with his hair flying in the wind. From her vantage point high above the meadow, she had seen the man dance with a little girl. She couldn't make out their faces, just the figures. She had watched with tears running down her face wishing it was her in his arms. Oh, what it would feel like to be cared about in that way. Many nights she would lay awake thinking about herself being loved by the king in the same way that the man loved that little girl. She had spied the man practicing swords with a boy. They would practice moves; the boy mimicking the man's every motion. Every session was the same. They all ended with the boy and the man play wrestling, rolling over and over in the tall grass of the meadow. The man would then carry the boy on his shoulders, pointing to different things.

The activities in the meadow, coupled with the images from her dreams had inspired many paintings over the last few months. Paintings that made her daydream about being a part of them. Paintings that made her think about visiting the king. But foolishness was what that was. All the stories she had been told as a little girl had been about how the king loved and played with the children. She had painted many images of the king and children, remembering them clearly from her dreams. But never did she hear stories of the king spending time with adults, let alone a crazy artist living on a hillside. The closest thing that was ever talked about was the young men trying to join the king's army, sadly, most returned. Nobody ever wanted to hear what the young men had to say. Many became successful in other things, but they hadn't been accepted into the army, so the town people looked down on them.

She closed her eyes and thought about what it would have been like if she had been born long ago. How exciting it would have been to run into the streets and see the king. This artist had such a great imagination. She pictured herself as a young girl having a tea party with the king, serving him cookies, sweetened tea, and freshly picked berries. As if in response to this deep longing, her hand grabbed the brush and started to paint a scene. But it wasn't of the tea party.

The brush swept frantically across the canvas painting the most elegant room. Large sets of French doors with sparkling glass were evenly spaced down two sides of the room. Around the doors, elegantly hand carved wood work appeared shiny and highly polished. Beautiful curtains formed a canopy above each set of doors with the curtains held back by golden wings. The floor was smooth, pearl colored marble with gold flecks. One set of doors was flung wide open and the king of her dreams stood with his arm stretched out welcoming someone in. He was dressed in a robe with sandals on his feet that were strung part way up his lower legs. Around his waist he wore a gold belt with a sword in its sheath attached. The simple gold ring which was around his head left little doubt that he was the king. Yet, its simplicity made the king appear kind and welcoming, not high and mighty like the town leaders acted.

The king's heart held a soft spot for this artist. She believed even when everyone had tried to convince her otherwise. She held strongly to the stories of long ago that her grandmother had lovingly spoken to her. She never doubted that the King loved his people. She knew deep down inside her heart that the king loved her. She just needed to be convinced that she was special to him as an adult, and that he longed to talk to her. The king's hand touched his heart and he caught his breath as the excitement flooded through him. It was time to make himself known to her.

The king slowed his horse to a trot and then a walk as he got closer. Before reaching the hillside artist, he slid off and left his mount to feed on the fresh grass under the trees as he walked to the edge of the clearing. He could see the small cottage where the artist lived surrounded by flowers and plants of various colors. The plants themselves looked like a living canvas as they swayed in the gentle breeze, the colors blending and contrasting, drawing the eye's gaze. The birds sang in harmony with the breeze as the nearby brook splashed on rocks to beat out a cadence. The king stood still enjoying the sights, sounds and smells that captivated his senses. He used to visit this place often. No wonder she had chosen here to paint.

Her brush moved toward the canvas to paint the next part, but she stopped it short. It could never be. A single tear escaped her eye and rolled down her cheek. She closed her eyes and stood still taking refuge in the sounds and smells of the hillside's nature. The longing in her heart, the deep desire to know, to really know the king became overwhelming. The world around her seemed to stand still as she became lost in her thoughts.

The king saw the tear and again touched his hand to his heart. He silently walked up behind her and saw what she had been painting. She had captured in every detail, the grand hall in his castle. Looking at the man in the painting was like looking in a mirror. His eyes, his expression, the curve of his mouth were identical to those in the picture. But fear had caused her to stop short. He reached his arms around her from behind in a gentle embrace. The time had come.

As she stood there she let herself imagine sinking into the arms of the king. These daydreams were becoming so intense that they seemed almost more real than reality. Maybe there was some truth to the words of the town people… crazy artist. She imagined her brush again moving to the canvas.

The king let her fall against his strong chest. He tenderly held her arm and raised the brush once again to the canvas. His long fingers slid over hers so softly that it was almost as if they were one. Together, they painted the final image onto the canvas. He guided her hand and added in the artist. She was standing in the doorway being welcomed by the king. She stood there with an amazing smile, and eyes that looked confidently in his direction. She was adorned in a deep purple gown. A lavender sash and jewels completed the ensemble. Her hair flowed from the top of her head, landing lightly on each shoulder and down her back. A shiny tiara was only partially visible in her hair. Tears ran down the king's cheeks as he realized his own longing to have this daughter as one of his own. He bent his mouth to her ear and whispered her name. Then ever so gently, lovingly, he commanded, "Wake up child, your time of longing is over."

She was so entranced with her heart's desire and a feeling of being loved that the sound of her name was almost unperceivable. But the voice that spoke it was somehow recognizable but unknown at the same time. She slowly opened her eyes and gazed for the first time into the face that she had so carefully painted all these years and deep in her heart she knew, this was the king. As she looked into his eyes, she knew she was accepted by the king. She followed his gaze to the canvas she had been painting.

The king loved this artist. Her heart had always yearned to know him. He grinned now as he watched her eyes. A sparkle of light glinted off the tears that formed in the corner of each eye. She reached out and grabbed the painting to see that it was real. There on the canvas was an image of her being welcomed by the king. She looked at the king, but words couldn't express the happiness, the contentment or any of the other emotions that swirled around inside her. He answered her puzzled look by saying, "We did it together, you were willing, and I was able." Then a deep hearty laugh erupted from his lips, as he said, "By the way, you painted me right" It was a contagious laugh that spread like wildfire. The two fell to the ground. Even nature seemed to have caught the joy and seemed to be laughing with them.

The beautiful hillside again became a spot the king visited often. Not just for nature, but to see one of his own. He commissioned the artist who he now called "Painting Right", to do some pieces to hang in the throne room. As news of this spread around the town, the townspeople started requesting paintings. She was no longer dubbed the crazy artist, but the king's artist. The king smiled, slowing his pace as he walked past one of her paintings. He had always known she would do great things. She just had to embrace her true identity and believe she was valuable.

4 SPREADING LIGHT

The atmosphere and attitudes around the kingdom were changing. The King was good and kind and had never stopped loving his people. Even when they pulled away from him, the king never abandoned the hope that they would one day welcome his presence in their lives. From his vantage point looking out the castle window, the king could see every building, every house, and every farm in his kingdom. He had planned it this way so he could watch over and protect his people. He glanced out now and watched the evening sun setting beyond the edge of his kingdom. He saw the smoke swirling up from the chimneys of many of the houses. The smoke seemed to dance and swirl on the fading pink, yellow and orange blends of the setting sun. It wouldn't be long now. Every night was the same routine and the king smiled as he waited, watching.

A man from the village kissed each of his children "goodnight". He hugged his wife as she snuggled on a chair with her favorite blanket and a good book. She smiled at him as he grabbed the guitar that leaned against the wall by the fireplace. He played a song for the kids every night before bed.

The guitar was old. It had been handed down in his family for at least three generations. The guitar had a clear resonating sound. It had been a gift from the king himself. The man's grandfather had given it to him when he was very young. The boy would visit his grandparents, pick up the guitar and play beautiful music. He never had lessons; it was as if he had been born knowing how to play. Recognizing his talent, he had been given the treasured guitar early on, being told, "Treasure it always and bring honor to the king when you play."

Every night, after the kids were snug in bed, the man would tend to the animals and then go off on his own to practice and write music and songs. The man smiled as he quickly fed the animals. He loved this life. He taught music to eager children at the town school. He had a beautiful wife and three energetic children. He thought back to the days of his youth when he had laid the guitar aside, replacing it with a sword. He had trained hard to join the king's army, but had found little joy and fulfillment in it. When he had finally met with the king, the truth could be hidden no longer. Those eyes, he would never forget the warm but penetrating eyes of the king. As he stood before the king, a tall, strong, good looking young man, he trembled in his boots. The king told him he had trained well. Then he asked him if he had enjoyed the training. He thought a moment about answering, "Yes". But then he looked into the king's eyes and the truth just trickled out, like water spilling from a cracked jug. There was no condemnation, only love. The king had sent him home, but not as a failure like the town thought. He came home with permission from the king to pursue his dream – music. The king had encouraged him by saying, "Don't despise small beginnings, but always remember who you are." And so it had all begun, and here he was now.

The town people didn't care about the king. They thought of him as an evil task master that demanded perfection. The man knew differently. He had begun writing songs about the king. All he had to do was think of those eyes and words that had been swimming in his mind fell into meaningful lyrics on the pages of the notebook he had hidden under his coat. He feared people's judgmental words so he kept them hidden, even from his family. But recently, the desire to sing these songs had taken on a sense of urgency that the man didn't quite understand. So here he was walking to the meadow to sing and play the secret music that had been birthed in his very soul.

There he was. The king smiled as he watched the man come out of the barn and walk down the dirt lane toward the meadow. The man had started this routine about a month ago. The king had noticed him one evening and had checked subsequent nights. It never ceased to amaze him. The man had an almost sheepish grin on his face. It reminded the king of the day when a young man stood before him and couldn't lie. He loved that about this man. Honesty rang true in him. He had worn that grin as he talked about his love of music. His voice rose with excitement as he talked about hearing music in his mind and then plucking out the notes on his grandpa's old guitar. The king knew the guitar well. He had played it in the early days of the kingdom, before giving it to a man much like this man. Both men marched to the beat of a different drum. This man just needed to know that it was an honorable calling. Tonight was the night; he would set things in motion.

A cool breeze was blowing gently as the man walked to his favorite spot in the meadow. The moon shone brightly, creating enough light to read and write. The light was of little concern to the man. He could play with his eyes closed. The music came from deep within his heart and worked its way to his fingers and then to the guitar. As the man began to sing and play, any onlooker would have agreed that the two were as one. The music rang out loud and clear and floated on the breeze and through the trees. The man lost all sense of space and time. He danced, jumped and moved with the music as if practicing some kind of warfare. The moon glinted off the guitar casting sparks of light around the meadow.

The king heard the music even before he reached the meadow. He stilled his horse and watched for a while. His heart beat in time to the cadence. Little did this man realize the effects of his music, so pure and innocent was the sound. The king likened it to a "call to arms". In the early days of the kingdom, the king had enlisted trained trumpeters to play a similar sounding cadence to call his knights to arms when it was time to go to battle. The king leaned back against a tree and just listened. The words brought tears to his eyes. The man was singing about the king. The words sounded like a glorious poem. They spoke of the king's love for his people, a love that never ended and couldn't be denied. The tears flowed as the king listened. The man got it; he knew and understood the heart of the king.

So lost in his music was the man that he didn't see or hear anything around him. He was fulfilling those words from long ago, "bring honor to the king when you play". In his mind he could see every detail of the king's face. The king was good. It was easy to sing about him. The king would truly be honored by this song. The man longed to be able to sing freely about the king to his children and to others. The town people shunned those who talked of the king in such ways. They had shunned the artist lady until the king commissioned her to do a painting for his castle. Tears welled up in his eyes but he managed to hold them at bay. The growing desire in his heart to see the king again, lined his music with passion.

The king caught glimpses of movement at the edges of the meadow and more over by the brook. And so it begins he thought. The king picked up two sticks and started playing percussion to the man's song as he walked toward him. As if on cue, other men picked up rocks to keep beat. Some started clapping or stomping their feet to the music. They too entered the meadow and formed "ranks" behind the man. The king now stood in front of the man, but said nothing. He had seen all these men at one time or another. These were the men that the town considered failures. Failures they were not. What joy they now brought to the heart of their king.

The man poured his heart, his soul, his life into this song. His conscious mind vaguely registered the percussion added to the music, but he was so involved with honoring the king that he didn't really pay it mind. As he finished playing the ending note, all became silent save a single voice speaking his name. He was jolted back to reality and feared what opening his eyes would reveal. But as his name was spoken again, he opened his eyes recognizing the voice, the voice of the king.

A smile spread across the king's face. "You have brought me honor and so much more" said the king. The man knelt before him and all the other men followed sync. It was then that he noticed them and turned his head. As the man looked at his friends and neighbors, he realized that he hadn't sung that song just for himself. He sang the words of longing that had long been hidden in all of their hearts. The man looked up at the king. The king drew his sword and lightly tapped first the right and then the left shoulder of the man. Then in an authoritative voice he said, "Rise up as an ambassador of the king. You will be called 'Spreading Light' for your music spreads the truth of my love for my people." All the men cheered. Then the king addressed those assembled there. "You all have brought me honor. Today each of you put aside your fear for my sake. I hereby commission all of you as knights and thus call you to arms. You are to do battle all around you. Speak of me to your families and friends. Tell of my love for my people. I want my people to come to know me again. You all have spheres of influence where you can make a difference. Some men fight with swords, I'm asking you to take up love and honor as your weapons of choice. Finally, stand firm."

With that the king whistled to his horse. In one swift smooth movement the king mounted and the pair sprang across the meadow amidst cheers and shouts. This army would bring change to the kingdom. The king grinned; wait till the children found out that their fathers loved the king, too.

5 WISDOM'S SIGHT

A vibrant glow radiated from the face of the king as he looked out the castle window toward the town. Glorious joy shone round about him. Oh, how he loved his people, and they were returning that love. A fire that had grown cold had sparked to life, starting with a small dancing girl, and then ignited in the dream of a young boy to serve the king. It continued to blaze in the heart of an artist who longed to know the king she painted, and was rekindled in the music that was birthed in the soul of a man who had met the king as a youth. Love's spark was becoming a blazing inferno, and the king was happy.

The old woman felt the warmth of the sunlight streaming through her cottage window as she approached. She inhaled deeply of the cool, fresh spring air blowing down from the mountains and across the meadow. A few more minutes and the last batch of cookies would be finished. The king would be smiling she thought as her mind replayed the events of the previous evening.

Her small cottage had been there practically forever. It sat quietly under the trees at the edge of the meadow on the outskirts of town. It was the first house you came to, but most people never saw it. They were so focused on the town or on their private discussions that they missed seeing the quaint little cottage with its barn and corral set back from the road on the right. She had lived there as a little girl and had raised her family there, preferring it and all its memories over the bigger homes in town center. She would run and meet the king in the meadow when she was little and had a deep loving relationship with the king. Over the years, she called herself his favorite, for she knew in her heart that what the king loved most about her was that which was uniquely her own.

She had seen the hearts of the town people grow cold and harden toward the king. She knew the king since he came and visited often over the years. She could recognize him just by his eyes, or the sound of his voice, or even the stride of his steps. She knew him well. The town people never even knew that their king was walking among them. This aged lady had seen the king at work. She was looking on when he helped a small child who had skinned his knee. The king helped him to his feet, touched the knee, and the scrape was gone. The child ran off to catch up with his friends. She was there when the farmer's wife gave birth. The infant was not breathing. A stranger happened by and held the small stillborn child. A few minutes later he breathed his first breath and let out a hearty cry. She had looked into the man's eyes – and she knew who he was. She had seen him on his many exploits, leaving a basket of food here, a small present there, some homemade bread with a jar of jam. He truly loved his people. Over the years she had come to keep a supply of baked goodies on hand. The king would stop by to enjoy a bite and some conversation before returning to the castle. He had come when her husband breathed his last. She saw the tears running down his chiseled cheeks. He held her as she cried and helped her replace the grief with joyful memories.

She had felt the tides changing these last few months. She would hear the voices of the children and the deep erupting laughter of the king. She knew the sound well and never tired of hearing it. She heard the clanging of swords as he trained the boy. She smelled the paint on his hands after he met with the artist on the hill. And last night was something she would never forget. Her cottage was dark except for a single flickering candle in her small bedroom. The breeze brought in a sound like none she had ever heard before. A strong deep voice sang of his king and the beat she heard was like a thundering cadence. She heard the man, the king, the declaration of honor, the cheers. The king had come by a short while later.

She heard the quiet knock and had let him in. He sat comfortably on the sofa by the fireplace as if he lived there. The king himself made her a cup of tea and sat with her. He knew she was almost blind these days and it didn't hinder her. She knew the house well, the town, and the people. She was called the town matriarch. Many were the words of wisdom that had been uttered from her lips. She had shared love and life with many of the town people. The king wanted to show her how special she was and what she meant to him. He touched her arm and she felt tingling all the way down to her heart. As he looked into her eyes, it was as if her eyes were opened. She saw more clearly than she had in years. She looked lovingly back at the king and rested peacefully in his strong embrace. He kissed her gently on her forehead and then spoke to her. "You are my favorite," he said. "I love that you know who you are and the gift that you are to others. I have seen you grow in confidence and grace. You have a tender heart and a love for my people. I want you to be a part of what I am doing." She looked at the king; knowing this truth deep in her heart. Hearing him say it to her was overwhelming. Tears flooded her eyes and she let them flow down her wrinkled cheeks. This is all she ever wanted, to be loved by the king. The king stood up and pulled her to her feet. He whispered in her ear, "I've been saving this dance for you." Fresh tears flowed. How did he know that she had long yearned to dance with him as the children did? She heard the king begin to sing over her and they danced right there in the living room. He sang of his love for her, his pleasure in her and his joy in this woman. Nothing in her life had filled her with such joy and contentment as this single moment. His finger brushed her soft cheek. "You have lived a life that reflects how much you love me. Your eyes may have grown old, but you see with wisdom and love. I am going to call you "Wisdom's Sight". Never doubt that you are valuable in my kingdom." They again sat down and the king said, "Let me tell you what I am going to do."

So here she was, baking cookies for the celebration. It hadn't taken long to enroll many of the town women to help. They had been talking about the king for some time. They had shared their own desires to fellowship with the king during a quilting circle. She had encouraged them to quilt a story square. The result was a quilt like they had never made before. Love was sewn into every stitch. They had been waiting for such a time as this, for the right time to give it to the king. Wouldn't he be surprised?

As the noon hour approached, the women gathered at the old woman's house. The men were assembled in the old barn by the cottage. The children were already in the meadow waiting for their play date with the king. They had no idea that their moms and dads would be coming to join them in the meadow. After all, the parents never came. This was going to be a great surprise.

The king was dressed in a bright white tunic with a gold sash. He smiled broadly from ear to ear as he rode proudly on the back of his horse. The children crowded round as he rode into the meadow. This had become the routine. The eager children would run up to greet the king and pet his horse. The king in return greeted each by name with a hug, hair tousle, or swing into the air. After the greetings, the king had the little ones hold hands and make a circle. He told them he had a special surprise for them.

The air reverberated with the mounting excitement. The king surprised the kids by putting two fingers in his mouth and whistling loudly. Right on cue, the men came marching into the meadow in perfect formation. Spreading Light started to sing and the other men joined in. Their deep voices sounded majestic as the sound vibrated off the trees and rode on the wind. The women followed behind them carrying plates of cakes and cookies. The children looked at their parents then at the king. They weren't sure what to think. Surprised and confused looks stared from the little faces. Then the king said, "I love everyone from the oldest to the youngest. You all are part of my family. Today we will celebrate because love has again overcome fear and shame in my kingdom. You each are special and called to be mine. What do you say to that?" The children broke out into shouts, laughter, and dancing. The meadow erupted into a grand celebration like the kingdom had never seen before. Families danced together and food was shared by everyone. The king didn't belong to just the children, or just the deserving ones, or just the strongest. He was there for everyone.

Everyone enjoyed time with the king. He spoke words of adoration and declaration over each man, woman and child. Painting Right gave a special painting to the king. It was a picture of him dancing with the children. The kids gave the king bouquets of hand-picked flowers. Then Wisdom's Sight brought the quilt to the king. Unashamedly he let his tears flow down his handsome chiseled cheeks. He was overcome with the love of his people. What pleasure this love brought to him, more joy than all the wealth in the kingdom. It was greater than all the deeds done to impress him or any victory ever won. His people finally knew how proud he was of them and understood his unfailing love. They knew their king.

It was quite late before parents started carrying sleeping children home. The spirit of joy lingered in the air and in their hearts and minds. The kingdom changed that day. The people called for their king and he visited them often. They stopped by the castle just to spend time with him. Town people stopped looking down on others. Instead, the people followed their heart's calling and shared freely of all that they were. They shared the king's love with one another. Joy flowed from each heart and the kingdom grew in love and prosperity under the protection of the king. And the king was indeed very happy.

ABOUT THE AUTHOR

Irene was born and raised in Massachusetts with her mom, dad, and seven brothers. She moved to Arizona where she met and married her husband, Don. They are the proud parents of four biological and three adopted children. Irene enjoys spending time as a family and spoiling her three grandchildren.

After serving as a children's pastor for fifteen years, Irene earned her degree in Elementary Education and is currently teaching 1st grade.

Writing is a hobby and publishing a book has been a dream that she is finally seeing fulfilled.

Made in the USA
Charleston, SC
30 July 2014